A THRILL OF HOPE

AN ADVENT STORY FOR KIDS

𝑓▸

THE FOUNDRY
KIDS

Kansas City, Missouri

Nervoucited

🔊 **NER-vuh-SIGH-ted**

adjective:

Being both nervous and excited at the same time

Think about these questions as you read:

1. What sort of things do you think Hope gets excited about?
2. What do you get excited about during Advent?
3. Read Luke 21:33 below. Why is it so exciting when Jesus says his words will never disappear?

Heaven and earth will disappear, but my words will never disappear.
Luke 21:33 (NLT)

Chapter 1

Ka-plow! Chicken feathers flew in all directions! Pieces of hay and chunks of broken wood floated back down to earth. Hope lay in the mess, staring up at the rafters of the stable, still wearing her trusty test pilot goggles. "That did not go as planned," she mumbled. She rubbed her aching elbow. "Nancy, what went wrong?"

Nancy was Hope's inventing partner. Nancy was also a cat, a very brave cat. Perhaps unreasonably brave. That's why Nancy had insisted on joining Hope on this test flight.

"Mrow," Nancy replied bravely. She twisted her neck trying to shake loose the chicken feather stuck between her eyes.

Hope laid on her back and thought. She thought about collecting chicken feathers every day for the past six months. She thought about picking out the wood, pulleys, and other gadgets from her pile of extra invention parts. She thought about tying it all together with leather straps from her dad's old sandals. She thought about strapping the wings to her back, climbing to the top of the stable, and leaping into the sky! Her Chicken Wing 3000 was a success! She was Chicken Girl, defender of the stable! She could fly!

Except she didn't. She fell. And it hurt.

Chicken Girl couldn't fly. Neither could Chicken Kitty. Nancy smacked a feather off her ear with her hind leg. "I wish I could do that," said Hope. "But I think my knee would fall off."

Hope started to roll over, but she heard a crackling, splintering sound. What did she break? Oh no. Not good. Maybe it was just a pile of sticks. Hope tried to remember what was on this part of the stable floor. All she could picture were feathers.

She started to roll over again. Crack. Splinter. Crick. Something was definitely broken, and it wasn't her elbow. She stood up. She looked down. She turned green.

The manger.

Hope and Nancy had landed right on the manger. But it wasn't a manger at all now. Now it was a pile of sticks. She was going to be sick.

Her parents were always super supportive of her inventing, but they didn't love it when Hope jumped off tall things and broke short things.

Just then, Hope heard the front door of the house swish open. She heard heavy footsteps. Then she heard her dad's voice.

"Hope!"

Chapter 2

"Hope!" Her dad stood in the doorway to the stable. "What are you doing?! Are you okay?"

"I'm okay, Dad. My invention to create chicken wings so people can fly just needs some more work."

"Hope," sighed her dad. He brushed feathers and hay and something that smelled really bad from her back. "Our chickens can't fly." *Now he tells her.*

"Listen, little chicky," her dad continued. "The census is tomorrow. People from all over the land are returning here to Bethlehem to be counted. Those people are going to need a place to stay. We've got rooms we can rent to them, but they're also going to need a place to put their animals. So, my brave and talented inventor, where do you think they will they put those animals?"

"In the stable," said Hope.

"And where will their animals get food?"

"From the manger."

"And where is the manger?"

Hope looked down. Chicken Girl had landed right on it, breaking it into a gillion pieces. That's what broke her fall. Saved by the manger. "About that, Dad . . . "

"There's no time to explain, Hula Hope. We need to prepare for our guests. I've got to clean the front entry, your mom is building a new table for one of the rooms, and your brother is running around feeding our own animals. That means you need to build a new manger before we have a barn full of donkeys and no place to feed them. That manger is very important to our little inn."

"Okay, Dad. Sorry. I'm on it." Hope's dad kissed her head and walked back out, pulling a feather from his ear.

Hope bent down and picked up some broken pieces of wood. She looked at the mess. She looked at Nancy. "Dad actually trusts me to build a new manger?" she said. "This is a big, important job! I can finally help the family with my inventions! I'm so nervoucited!"

She would rebuild the manger. Bigger. Stronger. Special . . . er. It would be great!

Hope was full of hope.

Chapter 3

"Nancy, it didn't work! Don't try it!" That cat was as fearless as Hope was resourceful. Nancy was a great inventing partner because she would try anything Hope created! "Nancy," Hope tried to speak calmly. "We already tried the Chicken Wing 3000. Remember? It was like seven minutes ago. That's why there are manger parts lying all over the place."

Nancy stared down at Hope from the rafters. She had on her own, cat-sized chicken wings. And she had that look in her eye.

"Don't do it!" Hope said again. "I can't spend time nursing you back to health after you break your tail or something. I've got to re-build this manger.

Fast!" The cat just stared at her. Nancy was unreasonably brave. But sometimes she was just plain unreasonable.

Turning back to the broken parts littering the floor among the feathers, Hope's brain began to buzz. She tightened her headband. She was in the inventor zone. The background began to fade. All she could see were the pieces of the manger fitting back together. This piece could be a leg. This piece could fit across the top. This piece could brace the bottom.

In a flash, Hope was skidding across the floor on her knees. She grabbed her hammer and nails. Her arms were a blur as she pieced together the broken manger. This piece fits! That piece fits! Hope measured and hammered, hammered and measured.

Finally, she stepped away from her creation. Using only the pieces from the broken manger, along with a few of her own gadgets, Hope had managed to build a brand new manger. "This one is even finer than the first," Hope thought.

Ka-boom! Her new manger exploded right before her eyes! Feathers, fur, and splinters flew in all directions. There, in the fresh pile of rubble, was her unreasonably brave cat named Nancy. She decided to try out her wings after all. Because, of course.

"Nancy! I just built this! Now it's even worse than before!"

"Mrow," came Nancy's reply. She stumbled off, looking a little woozy.

"You silly feline," said Hope.

Knock, knock! Hope heard pounding on the front door of the house outside. Her heart jumped. Was it already time? She heard her dad's voice. "Hello! What can I do for you?"

A man replied, "Do you have any rooms available?" Hope froze.

Chapter 4

Already?! It couldn't be time for guests to arrive! Hope scooped up Nancy and ran outside. Nancy was still licking feathers off of her back. Her dad was talking to the guests. "Of course! Of course! Let my son, Daniel, help you with your bags." He turned into the house. "Danny!"

Hope's older brother came running out. "Gotcha, Dad. Hey folks! I'll get you all set. Where's your donkey?" He looked at Hope and winked.

"No donkey," said the man. "Just a cart I pulled from Etam. It's there."

Hope let out a deep breath. She had caught a break. The first travelers to arrive didn't have a donkey or a camel with them! She still had some time to work on the new manger! She dropped Nancy, who slumped off toward the back of the stable. Hope ran after her.

She was going to need a plan. She couldn't rebuild the manger with wood from the first one. She tore the wood up with her flight—which was really just a fall. Then, Nancy had shredded it into toothpicks with her flight—which was also just a fall. Maybe the Chicken Wing 3000 needed adjustments to the aerodynamics. If she just tweaked the winglet drag . . .

"No!" Hope slapped the side of her head. "The Chicken Wing 3000 will have to wait! I need a manger!" She looked around. "I need a manger." She looked down, "I need a manger." She looked up, "I need a- aaaaahhh!!" Nancy came falling through the air with her chicken wings and little cat paws flopping like spaghetti noodles. Hope ducked out of the way. Nancy slammed into some hay behind her. Flumpf!

"Nancy, if you keep almost killing me, I'm never going to get this manger done!" Hope sighed and glanced around the room again. She noticed a broken cart in the corner. She pulled off a few pieces of wood. She grabbed a couple of gadgets from her tool box. She had what she needed. It was time to get started.

Chapter 5

Nervoucited. That's the best word to use. A few miles outside Bethlehem, walking along a well-worn path, was a nervoucited young couple. They had a big night ahead of them.

In town was an equally nervoucited little girl. She was wearing goggles, scurrying around a stable, and carrying a very determined-looking cat.

"What are you doing in such a rush?" Danny, Hope's brother, had poked his head through the stable window. "And why are you holding Nancy?"

"I'm building a new manger," Hope replied. "And Nancy can't be trusted."

"Chicken Wing 3000 didn't work, huh?"

"Well, I flew about as well as our chickens." Hope thought this was a nice way to put it.

Danny laughed. "Well, you're smart. You'll figure it out. Ooh, I know what you need!" In a flash, he was gone.

Nancy wiggled and fell to the ground. She ran off before Hope could catch her. Hope shrugged and kept working.

"Moooo," came the long, low bellow of Carissa the cow. She looked down at the broken manger. She looked at Hope. She looked upset.

"Sorry, Carissa!" Hope called over her shoulder. "I didn't mean to destroy your lunch box."

"Mrrroooowwwww!" Ker-flump! Nancy landed in the manger pile, sending sticks and feathers spinning toward the cow. Insulted, Carissa turned and walked away.

"And Nancy didn't mean to destroy it . . . again!" Hope said. "Nancy, we've established that you can't fly." Cats can't smile, but it almost looked like Nancy did. She tottered off.

"Hope!" She stopped quickly and tried not to drop anything from her armload as she turned toward the window.

"Yeah, Danny?"

"You might want this." Danny held out her pad of paper. It was filled with all of Hope's invention plans. "It might help you get your creative juices flowing."

"Thanks, bro!"

"You got it, Hula Hope." Danny looked at the mess of stuff in Hope's arms. "Uh, where should I put it?"

"Well," Hope said, "I guess you could-mmmrrrppphh!" Danny stuck the pad between Hope's teeth. Brothers.

"Thank you!" she called. Though it actually sounded like, "Aanngg yuuh." Hope turned around. It was time for an inventor's favorite phase: sketch dreaming.

Chapter 6

Manger #17
The Ba-Da-Bling

Thirty-seven. That's how many sketches Hope had drawn. Thirty-seven sketches. There was a tall manger. Great for the long-legged camels. There was a short manger. Stronger base for the heavy hogs. There was one with a lid that closed when Carissa had enough to eat. There was a manger that spun the hay. There was a manger on wheels. There was a bright pink, glittery manger. There was even a Chicken Wing 3000 Manger that could fly. Maybe she would try that one later.

There were so many ideas! Which one was she going to build?

"Which one do you like best, Nancy?" Hope looked back at the cat, but she wasn't lying next to Hope's feet. "Nancy?"

"Mrow!" Nancy replied from above. Hope looked up to see Nancy standing on the workbench. She had added extra feathers to her Chicken Wing 3000. She looked puffed up like a peacock. She jumped.

Blump! Nancy landed head-first into a bucket on the floor. The bucket spun twice and fell over. Nancy rolled out. "Extra feathers didn't work?" Hope asked.

"Mrow," Nancy answered. She danced, trying to free her tail from the bucket's handle.

Hope looked back at her drawings. She didn't have the glitter to make the pink one. She wasn't sure if she had enough wheels for the rolling one. She'd have to check. She quickly eliminated a few more options. She was getting closer and closer to building.

She began laying her supplies in rows. She had extra parts from the cart. She had extra leather leftover from her first Chicken Wing 3000 attempt. She had lots of feathers. (She wasn't sure how those would help.) She had nails. She had her tools. She had everything she needed.

Hope started to pick up her hammer, then put it back down. She reached for a saw, then put that back down, too. Her hand hovered over several tools and gadgets. She chewed on her bottom lip. Where should she start? Right now she was more nervous than excited. Hope jumped when she heard the door behind her creak open.

Chapter 7

"Dad! You scared me!"

"Sorry, little chicky." Hope's dad walked into the stable, shaking some feathers loose that were sticking to his sandal. "Just checking on your progress."

"Well, I've got all my supplies. I've got all my tools. I've got all my sketches . . ."

"Mrow!" Crash! Nancy bounced off dad's stomach and landed at his feet. Now there were even more feathers stuck in his sandal. Nancy looked up at Dad like she expected him to apologize to her.

Instead, Hope broke the staring contest. "Sorry, Dad, I've got a brave cat trying to fly like a chicken."

"Hope, our chickens don't fl-"

"I know, Dad."

Hope's dad walked over. "So, what are you waiting for?"

Hope looked down, "I've been so excited to build this, I think I've got my expectations built way up!"

Her dad nodded. "That's called 'anticipation.' It's a big word that means you're really looking forward to something. You're probably nervous and excited."

"I call that 'nervoucited'!" Hope announced.

Her dad laughed. "Nervoucited is a great word for it, too! You've been preparing for this. You've gotten yourself ready. You've done all this work in the advent of our guests arriving."

Hope wrinkled her nose. "Advent? What's advent?"

"Oh, advent means something is coming. And in the advent of something, we're preparing and anticipating."

Something amazing was definitely coming. Just a couple of miles away, the young husband was checking on his wife. She was pregnant, and getting weary. "We're getting close," he said. "I can see smoke from the fires in Bethlehem."

"Good!" Her voice was kind and tired. "I need a soft bed. And you know what I'm really craving? That quail salad with grapes in it that your mom makes."

"Oooh," her husband laughed. "Now I'm craving that too. Thanks a lot!"

Back in the stable, Hope's dad stood up. "You've been living in anticipation, girly. Now, you're ready to get started. Time is short. You've done everything you need to prepare!"

Hope nodded. "You're right. I'm ready. Thanks, Dad!"

"You got it, my great inventor." Dad walked out of the stable, still kicking feathers from his sandals.

Hope looked at her supplies. She closed her eyes. She took a deep breath. She reached for her first tool.

Zonified

🔊 **ZONE-if-eyed**

adjective:

Being completely focused on what you need to do

Think about these questions as you read:

1. What fun manger designs would you create if you were an inventor like Hope?
2. What does your family do during the Advent season that helps you to be zonified on Jesus's birth?
3. Read Luke 3:3 below. Why do you think baptism was so important to John? Why is it still important?

Then John went from place to place on both sides of the Jordan River, preaching that people should be baptized to show that they had repented of their sins and turned to God to be forgiven.
Luke 3:3 (NLT)

Chapter 8

Sawdust sailed through the air. Nothing was broken. Nothing was crashing. In fact, it was just the opposite. Hope was building. And she was good at it.

Her hands were a blur. She zipped around each side of the new manger. It was all coming together. She sawed, hammered, nailed, adjusted, tweaked, balanced, and then did it all again. Hope was zonified. Meanwhile, Nancy was sleeping. Face down. In a pile of hay. Sometimes brave cats are lazy.

Carissa was there too. But she seemed more hungry than lazy.

"I'm almost ready, Carissa!" Hope called out to the impatient cow. "Then we'll get you fed."

"Moo," said Carissa. That's pretty much all she ever said. Carissa's "moo" woke up Nancy and sparked an idea in her cat brain. She stood, stretched, and scampered off.

Hope reached for a few gadgets she had pulled from the old cart in the corner. A gear. A crank. An axel. These were perfect for this new and improved manger: The Stirminator 8800. That's the name she was thinking about. It would be a great invention. Her finest.

"Nancy, could you actually help out and hand me that socket wrench?" Hope looked over at where the cat used to be. "Nancy?" Hope looked up. "You're not jumping from the rafters and destroying another one of my inventions, you crazy cat!" Where was she?

"Mrow!" Nancy howled as she launched herself from the shadows of the rafters. Nancy was never going to stop trying to fly. And nobody was safe when she tried. This time her flight ended on Carissa's tail.

"Mooo!" cried the startled cow. She kicked her hind legs. Nancy tumbled through the air, and landed back on the pile of hay. Face down.

"Nancy!" Hope cried. "Are you okay?"

"Mrow," said the cat. She awkwardly tried to lick her back.

"Carissa, are you okay?"

"Moo." She looked offended. Carissa and Nancy weren't exactly best friends.

"Between the two of you, I'm surprised I've been able to get anything done at all! But I have!"

Hope stepped away from her new invention. It was finished. The Stirminator 8800. Hope had thought the moment would never come.

Chapter 9

"**Carissa,** what do you say? You want to give it a shot?" The cow looked positively giddy. Hope filled The Stirminator 8800 with hay from Nancy's nap pile. Carissa danced over to the new manger. Hope had never seen a cow look happier. "I guess you were getting a little hangry, huh?"

"Moo," Carissa replied. She was ready for dinner.

"Well, check out what I've done. See, I took these parts from that old cart over there, and I put them back together to create a stirring gadget for the hay in the manger. It attaches to the side, then I crank it like this." Hope turned the crank and the hay in the manger rustled as it was stirred by Hope's invention. "This will keep your hay fresh and never let any of it sit on the bottom for too long. What do you think, Carissa?" Hope beamed. It was nice for an invention to work right the first time.

"Moo," said the cow. She leaned in for a taste.

"Yes, please eat!" said Hope. Carissa began to munch. "See, and just like this, I'll stir the hay to keep it fresh!" Hope turned the crank.

"Mooooooooo!" Carissa bellowed. Hope looked inside The Stirminator 8800, and her eyes got humongous. Carissa's tongue was tangled in the mixer. "Moooo!" the cow shouted again. She tried to take a step backward but her tongue wouldn't budge.

"Aaah! Sorry, Carissa!" Hope yanked the crank the other way. The hay rustled and the invention released poor Carissa's tongue. The cow stepped away from the manger. Her tongue, now a few inches longer, flopped out of her mouth.

"Carissa, I am soooo sorry! I didn't know that would happen. I didn't even know my invention would work right in the first place! Can you ever forgive me?"

Carissa looked at Hope. "Muuuuthpthph," she said. Surprised, she stared down at her tongue. "Muuuuthpthph!" she tried again.

"Mrow, mrow, mrow!" Nancy made noises that Hope thought sounded like cat giggles.

"Nancy, stop that! Carissa, I'm sure your beautiful moo will be back to normal soon. Do you want another bite of hay?"

"Muuuuthpthph!" Carissa squealed, and backed quickly away from The Stirminator.

"Well, here's another invention that destroys things," Hope sighed. "Guess I'd better try again." She walked to her sketch wall and grabbed her next three favorite designs.

Chapter 10

Scraaape! Hope pushed The Stirminator 8800 against the back wall. She didn't have time to tear it down right now, and she wanted it out of the way so no one else got a tangled tongue. Carissa the cow looked cross-eyed at hers. Slurp! She tried sucking the dangling tongue back into her mouth.

Hope was certain one of these next three designs would be the perfect manger. There was just one problem. She couldn't decide which one to build. Since she didn't know which way to go, she decided to build them all. She kicked her inventing skills into high gear.

First, she built the Ultra-Comfort Manger 1200. Hope installed fluffy padding on the sides so the animals could rest their chins between bites. She attached an old rug to the feet of the manger. It gave the animals a soft place to stand while they ate.

She invited Carissa to test it out. "This is way better than The Stirminator. You'll love the padding. Promise!" Hope patted Carissa's back. "Just step up and enjoy your dinner!" The cow carefully stepped onto the rug, bent her head down, and took a bite of the padding.

"No, Carissa! Don't eat the padding!"

Startled, the cow spit out the fluff, danced quickly backwards, and slumped in the corner, tongue and padding hanging from her mouth. It was not a good day to be a cow.

Next, Hope created the Roll-A-Manger 360. This manger had the wheels from the old cart. Hope decided to give Carissa a break from being a test pilot and called out to her brother's donkey. "Gerald! Come try some hay from this new manger."

Gerald walked up to the manger and took a hearty bite. Maybe a little too hearty. The bite forced the manger to roll forward, away from the donkey. It rolled straight over Nancy's tail, ending her nap by the workbench.

"Mr-eeeek!" yelped the cat. She jumped, stumbled, and dashed out of the stable. It was not a good day to be a cat.

"Moohoohoo," said Carissa. Nancy thought it sounded like cow giggles. Gerald just stared at the hay that was now 10 feet away from him. He seemed to be asking for seconds.

Hope looked at her final drawing. Did she dare try another? No matter which way she went, she couldn't seem to get it right. She was running out of time.

Chapter 11

Hope knelt over her latest invention. Her mom walked by the window of the stable singing with a beautiful voice. It was the song she always sang while she was working.

"Look, your king is coming to you.
He is righteous and victorious,
yet he is humble, riding on a donkey—
riding on a donkey's colt."*

As she walked by she glanced in the stable and let out a low whistle. "You've been getting some work done, girl!" Mom and Hope fist bumped. Then she picked up the song where she left off, and set off to fix something else at the inn.

Hope thought this was such a catchy tune. It always got stuck in her head. She began to hum it as she worked.

"How's it going, Hula Hope?" Her dad walked into the stable, sizing up all the mangers Hope had made.

"I don't know, Dad. I've put together all these designs and not a single one has worked right."

"Hmm." Dad walked over to The Stirminator 8800. "What's up with this one?"

"It stirs the hay, keeping it fresh. It also catches cows' tongues and makes them talk funny."

Dad glanced over at Carissa, who seemed to nod. "What about that one? It looks comfy."

"Apparently animals can't tell the difference between the padding and the hay. And before you ask, Gerald took one bite out of the rolling one and almost flattened Nancy with it."

"Where is Nancy?"

"Mrow!" Nancy came flying through the air, feathers falling as she soared straight at him. Dad reached up and caught the cat before she did any damage. He held her up and looked her in the face. He was holding back laughter, but trying to look serious at the same time.

"You can't fly. Cats can't fly. Our chickens can't fly. You're going to break your tail, a manger, or your neck. Do you understand my words?"

"Mrow," was all the cat said. Hope wasn't sure if she understood or not. Dad patted Nancy on the head, sighed, and dropped her to the ground.

*Zechariah 9:9 (NLT)

Chapter 12

Nancy stretched her neck and licked her paw like nothing had happened. "Now you see what I'm dealing with around here?" Hope asked.

"Hope," Dad picked a feather from her hair, "You can't let these distractions get to you! Deep inside you know the way to go. You've got to be, to be . . ."

"Zonified?"

"Yes! Zoni . . . Uh, what's zonified?"

"It's what I call it when I'm in the zone. When I block everything out and focus on what I need to do. I know which way to go. I won't stop until I get there."

"That's it!" he shouted. "Zonified. You've got to get zonified!"

"Hope, is Gerald in here?" Danny walked in the stable.

"Yeah, sorry. I was just having him test one of my new mangers."

"Why are there so many? What does this lever do?" Danny turned the crank a couple times on The Stirminator 8800.

"Don't ask," Dad said, and pointed to the cow. Carissa looked away, offended.

Danny walked over to Hope. She was tinkering with the Roll-A-Manger 360. "Is that mom's song you're humming? I love that song," he said. Hope hadn't even realized she was humming again.

"Me too," she said. "It's catchy."

"You want to talk about being zonified?" Dad asked. Hope and Danny both looked up. "That song is about the Messiah coming. We are looking forward to the day he will come and show us the way to freedom! He'll know the way. In fact, he'll be the way."

"That song is about the Messiah?" Hope asked. "Isn't he supposed to be a king? Why would a king ride a donkey? Why not something fancy? I know! He could borrow my 450 Donkey-Powered Chariot invention!"

"Well, that's not exactly his style. If we pay attention to the Scriptures," said Dad, "we learn that he won't be like other kings. He'll be humble, kind, and full of love. And when he comes, he'll be locked in on showing us the way to God. Zonified."

"When do you think that will be, Dad?" asked Danny.

"When will the Messiah come? I don't know, son. But I hope soon. I hope really soon. In the meantime, Hope, you've got to get back to work. More guests will be arriving any time now!"

Danny jumped up. "C'mon, Gerald!" They trotted out.

"You've got this, Hula Hope," Dad said. And he left, too. Once again, Hope was alone with her tools.

Assemble this calendar with the gadgets found on page 63.

33

"**Yeesh.** Let me tell you a story, Nancy." Hope sighed. "It goes like this: Hope breaks a manger. Hope builds a manger. Nancy breaks a manger. Hope builds another manger. Carissa gets her tongue stuck. Hope builds another manger. Carissa eats part of it. Hope builds another manger. Gerald almost squishes Nancy with it." She looked at Nancy, "Great story, huh?"

"Mrow." Nancy wasn't sure what else to say.

Hope couldn't help but laugh at herself. Laughter helped her chill out. It helped her calm down. And she needed to stay calm. She had to stay zonified. She knew time was short. The next person could show up at their inn at any moment. She looked at the third sketch. She called it the MegaManger 4D. It was a triple-decker manger with swiveling baskets so lots of animals could eat at the same time. Did she dare start in on this one? Was this the way to go?

Hope heard a donkey outside. Gerald must be getting hungry again. Poor guy. He grunted again. Then she heard another Gerald. Wait. Another Gerald?

Hope's heart rate quickened. She climbed up to the window and peaked outside. People were lined up at the front door of their inn. Lots of people. Hope could hear her dad's voice over the noisy crowd. "Of course, we have several rooms left! Danny, can you get these bags? Hope, can you come out here please?"

Hope's heart sank. She didn't have the manger built. She bit her bottom lip and ran outside.

"Hope, these folks have a donkey that could use a rest in our stable."

"Sure, Dad." Hope took the donkey's reigns and smiled weakly. They smiled back. She looked at the line of people. She saw at least two more donkeys, and a camel.

Twenty minutes later, their inn was completely full of people. Their stable was completely full of animals. And Hope was completely full of despair.

She had to feed them all, and she didn't have a manger.

Chapter 14

"Hello." Her dad said. "What can I do for you?" Hope listened through the loose boards of the stable wall. The sun was fading.

"Hello, sir," came a man's gentle voice. "It took us longer to get into the city than expected. We're traveling a little slowly. My wife is going to have a baby anytime now. Do you have any rooms left?"

"Oh, I'm so sorry," Hope's dad sounded defeated. "We had a very busy run a bit ago. We have no room left. I even have people sleeping in the hallways."

"I understand," said the man. "Thanks anyway." They turned to leave. For the second time in 20 minutes, Hope thought she might cry.

"Wait," Dad said. "There's no room in the house, but we have a nice stable. It will at least get a roof over your heads. You're welcome to it. No charge. Just watch out for Nancy; she's one brave little cat." Hope swelled with pride.

"Oh, thank you, sir!" said the man.

"Hope?" called her dad. Hope ran to the door. "Our stable is going to have a couple of extra special guests tonight. Help them settle in, then come inside, okay?"

"Sure, Dad," said Hope. She watched the man, woman, and small donkey come to the stable door.

How could she have failed to make the right manger? Things did not go as planned. Her family would be so disappointed. She felt like a failure.

"Hi," said the young man. He had a kind face. "I'm Joseph. This is Mary."

"Hey kiddo," said Mary. "Looks like you keep a fine stable!"

"Well, not exactly fine," said Hope, looking at the ground.

"What's wrong with it?" Mary asked as she climbed off of their little donkey and scratched him under the chin.

Hope took a deep breath and blurted out, "I broke the manger earlier with one of my inventions and I haven't been able to fix it yet. Now I have all these animal guests and people guests and no manger for either of them!" She felt like crying. Again.

"An inventor, eh?" Joseph said. "Maybe I could help you. I'm no inventor, but I am a carpenter."

Shappy

🔊 **SHAP-ee**

adjective:

1. Being willing to share with a happy heart and attitude

2. Sharing happy, or happy sharing

Think about these questions as you read:

1. How many times do you see examples of sharing with a happy heart and attitude in Hope's story this week?
2. In what ways can you be generous to others with your time and talents?
3. Read Luke 3:10-11 below. How is this verse an example of being shappy? Can you think of other stories of Jesus's shappiness?

The crowds asked, "What should we do?" John replied, "If you have two shirts, give one to the poor. If you have food, share it with those who are hungry."
Luke 3:10-11 (NLT)

Chapter 15

"Carpenter?!" Hope shouted. "You're a carpenter?! I would love your help." Her problems came out in a gush, and the tears finally came. "I have tried to make so many mangers, and Nancy broke one, and then I almost broke the cow, and then Gerald almost broke Nancy, and then the donkeys and camels came, and then you got here, and now I'm crying and there's still no manger!" It felt good to say it all out loud.

"Oh, sweet girl!" Mary knelt next to Hope and put an arm around her. "Most kids I know couldn't even build one manger!" She looked around the stable. "It looks like you've built lots! You must be a great inventor!" She squeezed Hope, and reached down to stroke Nancy's head.

Hope sniffed. "I'm okay."

"You're more than okay," said Joseph. "You've got some real skills! You just need a little hand."

"You'd be willing to help me?" asked Hope. "You must be so tired from your trip from . . ."

"Nazareth."

"Nazareth! We have family there! Isn't that like five days from here?" asked Hope.

"More like seven days when you have a slow beast like this one," said Joseph, pointing over at their donkey.

"Champion isn't slow!" said Mary, scratching the donkey's chin. "He's just patient."

Joseph rolled his eyes and smiled. "He's the slowest donkey on earth. At times I thought we were moving backward," he whispered to Hope. She giggled.

"I heard that!" said Mary. She pointed at Joseph. "Oh!" she said suddenly, and put a hand on her round tummy.

"Uh oh," said Joseph. "I think it's almost go time with that baby. Mary, sit and rest. Hope, if we're gonna get you a manger built, we'd better do it quick!"

"You still want to help me build a manger—even after that long trip and with Mary about to have a baby?"

"Hey, I'm shappy to help," he said, putting out his hand for a high five.

"Shappy?"

"Oh, it's a word I made up when I was a kid," said Joseph. "It means I'm willing to share, and I'm happy to do it. Sharing happy. Shappy."

"I make up words, too!" shouted Hope. She knew she was going to like Joseph.

"Well now, let's make up a manger!" said Joseph.

Hope grabbed his hand and led him to her wall of sketches.

Chapter 16

"Wowza!" said Joseph. "That's a lot of mangers."

Hope was nervoucited to show him everything she had worked on. "This one shoots the hay into the cow's mouth using a foot-propelled launching gadget. This one stirs the hay into a smoothie and even drops in a straw. And this one . . ."

"Mrow!" shouted Nancy. She came flying from the top of the workbench, bounced on Joseph's shoulder, and backflipped into the padding of the Ultra-Comfort Manger 1200.

"What in the world was that?!" Joseph shouted as he jumped and flung his feet like he was about to fight an army of ninjas.

Mary laughed from across the stable, then held her tummy again.

"That was Nancy." Hope giggled. "She's using one of my inventions. It's supposed to help you fly like a chicken. She keeps trying, and it keeps not working. She's unreasonably brave."

"Oh," said Joseph. "I guess I'm a little on edge with everything going on. Let's get that manger built!"

"Which one should we do?" Hope asked.

"Well, there's something special about all of these," he replied. "But given that we really only need it to do one very important job, do you think we could go for a really simple design?"

"Like what?" Hope asked.

"Could I use your notebook for a minute?"

Hope handed Joseph the sketchbook and he began to scribble. Then he turned it around and held it up. "How about this?"

"But, there are no cranks, axels, swiveling arms, or chicken wings on it," Hope replied.

"Er, no. But there are good sturdy legs and plenty of space to hold the hay. It's not fancy, but it'll do exactly what we need it to do!"

Hope sighed. "Let's hope you're right." She grabbed her tools and brought them over to Joseph. He took a saw. She took a hammer. Ten minutes later, they stood up.

"Let me see!" said Mary from across the room. "Champion, scooch over."

Joseph announced, "Presenting the . . . ," he knelt down and whispered to Hope, "What do you want to call it?"

Hope bit her lip, then answered, "The Manger."

"Simple. Humble. I like it." He winked and stood back up. "The Manger!"

"Yay!" Mary clapped. "It's perfect!" Then she winced. "Oooh. Hey Joe?"

"Yeah, hun?" he said smiling.

"I think it's baby time."

Chapter 17

"**Baby time!** It's baby time!" Joseph ran to the door of the stable. Then he ran to the window. Then he tripped over Nancy who was scrambling to get out of his way. He fell in the dirt, then picked up the cat. He looked her right in the face. "It's baby time!"

"Mrow!" Nancy shouted back. She was either caught up in the excitement, or scared for her life. Joseph dropped her and she quickly scrambled under the workbench. Scared for her life. Not so brave now.

"What should I do?!" shouted Hope.

"It's baby time!"

"Joseph, calm down. I need your head in the game!" Mary was waving at her husband from her seat in the hay.

"Get zonified!" Hope shouted. "I got him!" She grabbed the Roll-A-Manger 360, watched Joseph scramble back and forth for a second, then shoved it toward him. Her timing was perfect. The Roll-A-Manger hit Joseph in the back of the legs, knocking his feet out from under him. He landed in it as it continued its path, stopping a foot away from Mary. Champion looked at Carissa. They both rolled their eyes.

"Joseph," Mary gently grabbed his face and turned him to look at her. "The Messiah is coming." Joseph stared at her, and then slowly nodded.

What did Mary say? Hope must not have heard her right. She cleared her throat. "Uh, what can I do?"

"Oh, Hope. You have done so much to help us feel comfortable here. You even gave Joseph a job to keep his mind distracted. If you can't tell, he's a little worried about having a baby."

"In a barn!" Joseph shouted. He looked at Hope. "Sorry, Hope. It's a great stable."

"Hey, no sweat," said Hope. "I wouldn't want to have a baby in a stable either. Can I help you guys?"

"You'd better . . . yeeeiiikes!" Mary started to talk, but then held her tummy again. "You'd better do what your dad said. You've got the animals settled with their new manger, and we're in for the night. Head on inside, sweetie."

Hope wanted to protest. She wanted to stay. But she needed to obey her dad. Mary was right.

"Alright, I'll head in. I'll check on everything later."

"Thanks, Hope," said Joseph. He was getting a blanket off of Champion. Hope walked out the door. What did Mary say about the Messiah?

Chapter 18

"**Pssst,** come on Nancy!" The cat bounded out of the shadows, a few chicken feathers floating behind her. "We need to go in." Hope picked her up.

Inside was a madhouse. There were people staying in what seemed like every extra inch of their house. "Excuse me," Hope said as she stepped over a lady holding a bowl of soup in the hallway.

"No problem, deary," said the lady.

Hope slipped into the kitchen, where her dad was handing a mug of something warm to another man. "It's my wife's special tea," he was saying. "I don't know what's in it, and I don't ask. But it makes me feel 10 years younger!"

"Just what I need after four days on the road," said the thankful man.

"Hula Hope!" her dad turned to her. "How's the stable looking?"

"Everything's all set, Dad." Hope was distracted, knowing Mary and Joseph were out there.

"And your new manger?"

"I got it done, but only because Joseph came in and helped. He's a carpenter! He said he was shappy to do it."

"Shappy? That sounds like one of your words!"

"That's what I thought. It means happy to share. He made it up."

"Ah, like generosity, huh? If you're generous, you not only share with people, you do it with a willing attitude."

"Definitely like that, Dad. Joseph was very generous with me," Hope said.

"I sure hope they're okay out there. Do they need anything?"

"They told me they were fine. They sent me inside."

"Well," said Dad, "you've done a fine job today, little chicky." He pulled a feather from Nancy's fur. "You'd better get ready for bed."

Hope went upstairs to her room, but there was no way she could sleep. She sat by her window and looked down at the stable roof. "You think they're okay in there, Nancy?" Hope looked down. "Nancy?" She turned around. Her unreasonably brave cat was perched in the window with her chicken wings, getting ready to leap. Hope lunged and grabbed her. "No you don't! We're too high up, you wacky feline."

"Mrow," Nancy replied. Her bravery was back.

"Quiet, Nancy!" Hope stuck her head out the window. "Do you hear that?" Nancy cocked her head. "It sounds like . . . a baby."

Chapter 19

"Nancy! What do we do? What do we do?" There had never been a baby born in Hope's stable before. Nancy watched Hope run back and forth across the bedroom. "I need to take something to the baby. A gift. Something to help it stop crying." Hope felt panicky. She opened her door and shouted, "Danny!"

Danny was coming up the hallway. The house was growing quiet. "Shhh, Hope! This place is finally starting to settle down! I've parked more carts and carried more packs than I can count, and now I just need everyone to sleep!"

"Sorry. Uh, quick question, what did I like when I was a baby?"

"What?" Danny smiled. "Random, Hula Hope. Super random. Why?"

"Uh, I just need to know." Hope didn't know if Mary and Joseph were ready for extra visitors, so she didn't want to tell Danny about the baby yet. Surely they'd be fine if she came down, though.

"Well, let me think, when you were a baby . . ." Danny looked at the ceiling. He scratched the little tuft of beard he was trying to grow. "Oh, I know. You had a little stuffed lamb. You carried it around with you everywhere."

He meant Larry. Larry the lamb still lived on Hope's bed. She didn't remember a time in her life without Larry. She loved him. She also couldn't imagine what it would be like to be a baby in a barn. Dirty. Stinky. Chilly. Feathery. Lonely.

"Thanks, Danny. G'night!" Hope shut the door. She grabbed Larry without a second thought. She stuck Nancy under the other arm and slipped out. She stepped over a man snoring on the floor, and ducked under another who had hung his hammock from wall to wall.

Hope tried to be quiet as she bobbed, hopped, and tiptoed through the maze of people filling their inn for the census. How she wished her Chicken Wing 3000 worked right now! She almost slipped up when she dropped Larry in a sleeping woman's open mouth. She quickly grabbed the lamb and wiped it off. Yuck! The woman coughed and turned over, but didn't wake.

Somehow, Hope made it outside. She could definitely hear the sounds of a baby just a few feet away. She took a deep breath, and walked into the stable.

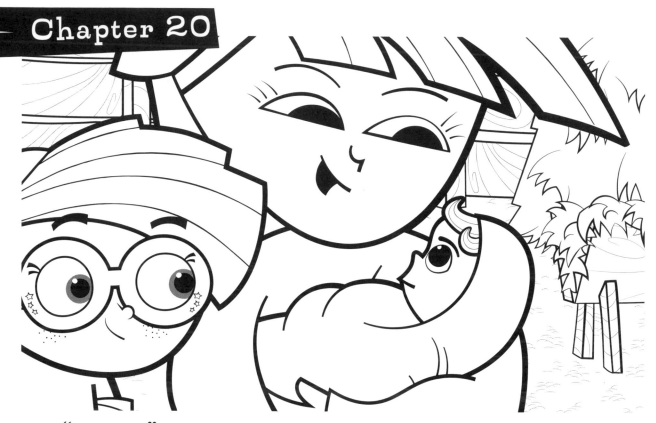

Chapter 20

"Hope!" Joseph stood when she walked in the door. "Do you want to meet Jesus?"

"Jesus? You named him Jesus?"

"Well, we didn't really choose it. An angel told us to. But we like it."

"Oh, well that's . . . did you say 'angel'?!" Hope was confused.

"It's a long story," Joseph chuckled. "Come, come!"

Hope walked toward the baby. She stepped carefully. The whole stable somehow felt different. Special.

"Hi, Hope," came Mary's gentle welcome. She was holding a bundle of cloths. Hope thought the baby must be stuffed in there somewhere. "Come see."

Hope knelt next to the young woman and looked into the cloths. She saw a little patch of dark hair, brown skin, and finally, dark brown eyes. Jesus. Hope held her breath. She could tell this baby was special.

Suddenly, a thought struck her. She jumped to her feet. "Where will he sleep?!" Hope whisper-shouted. "You need a bed! I've got one up in my room. I'll drag it down here. Nancy can help me pull it." Nancy looked up, startled at being volunteered to do heavy lifting, and ran off into the shadows. "No wait, it's too big. Gerald can come up and help me! And Champion! We'll bring it down. And blankets!" She was out of breath.

"Hope, it's okay," Mary gently laughed. "Your house is full of sleeping people."

"But he needs a bed!"

Joseph looked around, "You know, Hope. You built a mighty fine manger over there. It's full of soft hay. Think that would work?"

"You want to use my manger? Our manger? That manger?"

Joseph nodded. "Yes. It'll be perfect. Can you pull it over here?"

Hope ran quickly to the manger she and Joseph had built. She dragged it as quietly as she could to Mary's side. Mary spread out a blanket on the hay and placed the now sleeping baby in it. "It's perfect, Hope. Thank you."

"Almost perfect," said Hope. She lifted up Larry and placed him next to the baby. "This is Larry. He's my lamb. I want little baby Jesus to have him."

Mary looked like she was about to cry. "Hope, that is such a generous gift. A gentle little lamb is perfect for our Jesus."

"Well, I'm shappy to do it," said Hope. They all laughed.

Chapter 21

Angel. Messiah. Hope needed answers. They all sat looking at Jesus. "Hey, Joseph? Uh, who did you say named the baby?"

Joseph laughed. "I know it sounds crazy, Hope, but an angel, one of God's messengers, appeared to both Mary and me! The angel told us to name him Jesus and that he will be a great king, the Son of God, and that his kingdom will never end. He will save us all."

"A king?!" Hope was shocked. "But he's in a stable, sleeping on some hay, surrounded by donkeys, camels, and Carissa! How can he be a king?"

"Well, he's not going to be like other kings," Joseph suggested. He leaned in and whispered, "From everything the angel has told us, we believe Jesus is the

Messiah. Do you know about the Messiah?"

The lessons Hope had learned from her parents came to her in a rush. "The Messiah will be a king, but he'll be humble, kind, and full of love. Not like other kings," Hope quoted her dad. "Oh, and my mom sings a song about him being a humble king." Hope glanced down at the dirt floor. "I think he's already got the humble thing figured out."

"That's true," Joseph smiled. "He won't come from a place most people think is important. Just a carpenter's boy, born in a stable. That's humble."

"But he's sleeping in a very nice manger," Mary added.

Hope blushed. "This is really the Messiah?" Even as she asked, she knew it was true.

"God, right here with us," Mary said. "And Joseph and I get to raise him. It all sounds so big and crazy when I say it out loud."

Hope looked at the dirty old stuffed lamb next to the baby. "I don't think Larry is a very good gift for God's Son."

"Oh, Hope," said Mary, "Larry is a wonderful gift! In fact, you have been generous with us at every turn."

"Shappy," nodded Joseph, as he munched on some dried figs.

Mary agreed. "You welcomed us into your stable. You built us a manger bed, and you gave Jesus Larry the lamb."

"I guess," said Hope. She was still unsure.

"I know it," said Mary. "God is generous with us, giving us hope through Jesus. You have been generous with the Son of God. Generosity has been your way, Hope. And generosity is the way of hope."

Keepster

🔊 **KEEP-stir**

noun:

A promise that has been kept

Think about these questions as you read:

1. If you were visited by an angel like Joseph and Mary, what questions would you want to ask?
2. How do you think Mary felt when she was told she would be Jesus's mom?
3. Read Luke 1:45 below. What big promise does God keep in this story? What other promises has he kept for you?

You are blessed because you believed that the Lord would do what he said.
Luke 1:45 (NLT)

Chapter 22

"Look," Joseph said, still chewing his snack. "I'm just a carpenter. But getting visited by an angel gets you thinking, so I did some research. Hundreds of years ago, the prophet Isaiah said someone just like Mary would have a baby. The prophet Micah said the baby would come from Bethlehem. Isaiah said he will rule forever and he will be God right here with us."

Hope was fascinated. People were telling stories about this baby—this cute little baby asleep in her manger—years and years before he showed up tonight! How could they know? It felt like Carissa's tangled tongue and Nancy's chicken flights were ages ago. It was like Hope lived in a brand new world, and this baby was the center of it.

"These men were God's messengers. Prophets. And God was promising that the Messiah would come," Joseph finished.

"Oh," said Hope, "then he's a keepster."

Joseph looked surprised. "What's a keepster?"

"It's my word for a promise that gets kept. The Messiah was promised, and here he is. Promise kept. Keepster."

"I love that," Joseph beamed.

"So it makes sense that the angel would want us to name him Jesus," said Mary.

"Why?" Hope asked. "What does Jesus mean? Wait, let me guess," she looked around and grinned. "Jesus means . . . born with donkeys?"

Joseph was taking a drink and water shot out of his nose. He laughed and coughed and brushed off the front of his robes. Mary was laughing too.

"No, no, it has nothing to do with donkeys," Mary said.

"Stable king?" Hope guessed. "Manger baby? Uh, cute little . . . God child?"

"You're getting closer. Joseph?"

"Savior," Joseph said. His love for Jesus was clear. "Jesus means Savior. He's the bringer of hope."

"How will he save us?"

"Well, everyone thinks the Messiah is supposed to rescue us like a mighty warrior with a sword. But this king was born in your manger instead of in a palace. He's going to rescue everyone with his love. He'll bring hope to the world so that we can have victory over bad things. Remember how you hoped to build a fancy manger, but this simple one ended up being exactly what we needed? Everyone's hoping for this fancy king, but this little baby right here is exactly what everyone needs."

Chapter 23

The stable was quiet. Nancy didn't try to fly. Hope didn't try to build. Joseph finally looked like he could relax. Mary sat, thinking about everything that had happened. They all stared down at the miracle before them. Savior. Messiah. Keepster. God, right there with them. A real person. For a moment there wasn't anything to say. For a moment, just being there at Jesus's side was enough.

Chapter 24

Nervoucited. That's how Hope had felt when she was asked to build the manger. She looked forward to it with anticipation. She could not have known she was really building the Savior's bed! She was glad Dad gave her the pep talk he did. She was then zonified enough to finally get the job done, even though it didn't happen the way she expected. She was getting used to the idea that things with Jesus weren't always going to go as expected.

She was glad Joseph taught her his word, shappy. It was a perfect way to describe how she felt about helping Jesus. God was shappy to give us Jesus. Hope was shappy to give him a manger and Larry.

Knock, knock. Hope looked up at the door. Who could be here now? It was late. A boy about Danny's age poked his head in and looked around. His eyes landed on Jesus. He looked at Hope. "Is that him?"

"Is who him? Who are you? Who is him?" Hope was confused.

"The angels said he would be wrapped up in cloth and lying in a manger. That's gotta be him," said the boy.

Joseph stood up, "And who are you?"

Mary placed her hand on Joseph's arm. He looked at her, and then sat back down. Mary looked at the boy. "Yes," she whispered. "It's him."

"It's him!" the boy shouted to someone outside. Five more young men came running in, talking to each other. "We were in the field," said the boy, "and angels—real angels . . ." he trailed off.

"We understand," said Mary. "Meet Jesus."

"Mrow!" Nancy's cry cut through the night. She sailed from the rafters with her cat-sized Chicken Wing 3000 strapped to her.

"Oh no," said Hope. "Not again."

Nancy swooped toward the shepherds, curled upward, and backflipped in the air. She was . . . flying! The invention worked! Her wings flapped as she curled around their heads and landed on the young shepherd's shoulder. He stared at Nancy in surprise. "Uh, your cat can fly?"

Hope laughed. "I guess so!"

"That's crazy!" said the shepherd. "What's your name?"

"Oh, my name's Hope. But don't worry about me." She pointed at Jesus. "That's just my name. But this baby, he is hope."

The Advent Calendar is right in the middle of this book on pages 32-33. You'll find a picture of a stable with a lot of missing gadgets. Don't worry. All of those missing pieces are right here!

Locate the gadget on page 63 after you read each day. Chapter numbers are on the back of each gadget.

Cut out the gadget along the dotted lines on page 64.

Find the matching chapter number on the Advent Calendar (pages 32-33).

Glue or tape the gadget in its spot.

Color the gadgets and calendar as you go.

Enjoy watching the Advent Calendar fill up as Christmas gets closer!

63

<table>
<tr><td>1</td><td>10</td><td>11</td><td>20</td><td>21</td></tr>
<tr><td>2</td><td>9</td><td>12</td><td>19</td><td>22</td></tr>
<tr><td>3</td><td>8</td><td>13</td><td>18</td><td>23</td></tr>
<tr><td>4</td><td>7</td><td>14</td><td>17</td><td rowspan="2">24</td></tr>
<tr><td>5</td><td>6</td><td>15</td><td>16</td></tr>
</table>